For Dad, lover of all the wild things —L.G.S.

For Rebecca and Teasel —C.G.

My thanks to Dave Mech at the International Wolf Center and Kira Cassidy at the Yellowstone Wolf Project for their generous guidance and expertise. —L.G.S.

G. P. PUTNAM'S SONS
An imprint of Penguin Random House LLC, New York

First published in the United States of America by G. P. Putnam's Sons, an imprint of Penguin Random House LLC, 2023

Text copyright © 2023 by Liz Garton Scanlon | Illustrations copyright © 2023 by Chuck Groenink

Visit us online at penguinrandomhouse.com.

Library of Congress Cataloging-in-Publication Data
Names: Scanlon, Liz Garton, author. | Groenink, Chuck, illustrator.
Title: Full moon pups / by Liz Garton Scanlon; illustrated by Chuck Groenink.
Description: New York: G. P. Putnam's Sons, 2023.
Identifiers: LCCN 2022003552 (print) | LCCN 2022003553 (ebook) | ISBN 9780525514558 (hardcover) | ISBN 9780525514565 (epub) | ISBN 9780525514589 (kindle edition)
Subjects: CYAC: Stories in rhyme. | Wolves—Fiction. | Animals—Infancy—Fiction. | LCGFT: Stories in rhyme. | Animal fiction. | Picture books.
Classification: LCC PZ8.3.S2798 Fu 2023 (print) | LCC PZ8.3.S2798 (ebook) | DDC [E]—dc23
LC record available at https://lccn.loc.gov/2022003552
LC ebook record available at https://lccn.loc.gov/2022003553

Manufactured in China

Special Markets ISBN 9780593856321 Not for resale

1 3 5 7 9 10 8 6 4 2
RRD

Design by Marikka Tamura | Text set in Narevik Bold | The art was done in gouache, acrylics, pencils, oil pastels, and digital media.

FULL MOON PUPS

BY Liz Garton Scanlon

ILLUSTRATED BY Chuck Groenink

putnam

G. P. Putnam's Sons

A wind whips up the forest,
the sky is full of moon,
and Mama Wolf is restless,
with her litter coming soon.

Fox slips through the brambles
while midnight shines on Owl,
and after many hours
comes Mama's tired howl.

Now here they are—her babies—
protected in their den.
She licks them as they whimper
and pulls them close again.

These first few days, they're nursing.
They sleep and scootch and cry,
with the wolf pack watching over
like the moon does from the sky.

The pups, still blind but crawling,
start to feel their way around.

Tiny paws find roots and rocks
but hardly make a sound.

A storm comes out of nowhere,
and the world swells wet and gray.
For days, the water rises—
it could sweep the pups away!

The older wolves come loping,
gather pups up in their mouths,
and take them far from danger,
higher up and farther south.

Safe in their new nursery,
they open up their eyes
underneath a moon that's waning,
just a scoop there, way up high.

And then it's gone completely.
The sky's a heavy black,

not a sparkle or a glimmer—
hackles rise upon arched backs.

Noises come from everywhere.
Who's hiding in the dark?

A snap of branches, flash of wings;
the wolf pack bays and barks.

The pups grow ever bolder.
They start to reach and range.
What is that? And who is this?
The whole wide world is strange!

Days go by so quickly
as they tussle, tumble, hide.
Their floppy ears begin to lift.
Their eyes shine bright and wide.

Each night brings new surprises—
a wrestle or a roar,

a bit of meat from Mama,
and moonlight more and more.

Until it's full and round again,
a promise made complete
to this pack of waxing wolf pups,
who stand yipping at its feet.

Voices high and necks outstretched—
such mighty shadows thrown!
But it will be many moons still
till these pups are fully grown.

AUTHOR'S NOTE

I grew up in the Rocky Mountains, far from any city. We frequently saw wild creatures like marmots, coyotes, and bighorn sheep, but we didn't see wolves. Hundreds of thousands of wolves used to range North America, but as human development increased, the wolves' habitat shrunk. Plus, in the early twentieth century, there was an effort to exterminate wolves because they were seen as a threat and a nuisance. By the 1930s, wolves were on their way to becoming extinct in the contiguous forty-eight states.

Since then, scientists have demonstrated the value of wolves in a balanced ecosystem. As predators, wolves keep populations of deer, elk, moose, and coyotes in check, and their kills help feed scavengers and enrich the soil. Fortunately, wolves have made a good recovery thanks to the legal protection they received from the Endangered Species Act, which banned hunting them or damaging their habitats. A reintroduction effort helped, too, by settling gray wolves from Canada back into their historic rangeland in the United States.

The wolves in this story are some of those reintroduced animals—gray wolves living in or near Yellowstone National Park. In Yellowstone, wolf packs are again part of a successful and interconnected ecosystem, and they enjoy plenty of protected territory in which to dwell, hunt, and breed.

After mating, a female wolf will carry her pups for a little over two months. During that time, she selects a den—a cave, a hole in the ground, or even a hollow log—where she'll give birth to a litter of tiny, crying creatures. In just a matter of weeks, those pups go from being blind, deaf, and completely dependent on their mother, to walking, wrestling, and even chewing little bits of meat. By the end of the month, their ears perk up, their vision sharpens, and they make their first high-pitched howls by the light of the moon, which changes along with them all month long.

THE PHASES OF THE MOON

The moon doesn't produce any light of its own. We can see it in the night sky because it's illuminated by sunlight that reaches the moon even when it can't reach us. Because the moon travels in an orbit around the Earth, its appearance changes a little each night. As the moon gets fuller and brighter, we say it is waxing, whereas a waning moon grows slimmer and darker in the sky.

| new moon | waxing crescent | first quarter | waxing gibbous | full moon | waning gibbous | last (third) quarter | waning crescent |

The lunar cycle takes just under a month to complete. If a litter of wolf pups were born on the very night of a full moon, they would be getting big, bold, and playful by the time the moon completed one whole cycle. Wouldn't that be fun to see?

SELECTED BIBLIOGRAPHY

Blakeslee, Nate. *American Wolf: A True Story of Survival and Obsession in the West*. Crown, 2017.

Lopez, Barry. *Of Wolves and Men*. Scribner, 1978.

Smith, Douglas W., Daniel R. Stahler, Daniel R. MacNulty. *Yellowstone Wolves: Science and Discovery in the World's First National Park*. University of Chicago Press, 2020.

INTERNET SOURCES

International Wolf Center
wolf.org

Wolves in Yellowstone National Park
nps.gov/yell/learn/nature/wolves.htm

Defenders of Wildlife Gray Wolf Fact Sheet
defenders.org/wildlife/gray-wolf

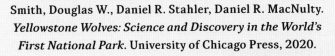